Superphonics® Storybooks will help y[ou] learn to read using Ruth Miskin's hi[gh] phonic method. Each story is fun to read and has been carefully written to include particular sounds and spellings.

The Storybooks are graded so your child can progress with confidence from easy words to harder ones. There are four levels - Blue (the easiest), Green, Purple and Turquoise (the hardest). Each level is linked to one of the core *Superphonics® Books*.

ISBN: 978 0 340 79893 5

Text copyright © 2002 Gill Munton
Illustrations copyright © 2002 Neal Layton

Editorial by Gill Munton
Design by Sarah Borny

The rights of Gill Munton and Neal Layton to be identified as the author and illustrator of this Work have been asserted by them in accordance with the Copyright, Designs and Patents Act 1988.

First published in Great Britain 2002

10 9 8 7 6 5 4

First published in 2002 by Hodder Children's Books, a division of Hachette Children's Books, 338 Euston Road, London NW1 3BH An Hachette UK Company. www.hachette.co.uk

Printed and bound in China by WKT Company Ltd.

A CIP record is registered by and held at the British Library.

Target words

All the Green Storybooks focus on the following sounds:

Double consonants,	Blended consonants,
e.g. **ll** as in **hill**	e.g. **ng** as in **long**

Two or three consonants together, e.g. **gl** as in **glad**, **nd** as in **band**

These target words are featured in the book. Some of them are nonsense words, but as they are phonically regular they provide useful practice.

buffacat	wallaphant	deck
cross	will	getting
fizz	yell	jumping
glass	along	kicking
grass	asking	long
gruff	back	neck
hill	black	pong
spells	brick	sick
tell	chuck	singing
terrabat	dancing	sitting

things	grim	slam
whack	grump	slump
wrong	jump	stamp
	just	stink
and	hand	strut
band	hump	think
best	pandapin	trunk
catch	patch	went
frog	sandwiches	witch's
glad	skin	witches

(Words containing sounds and spellings practised in the Blue Storybooks have been used in the stories, too.)

Other words

Also included are some common words (e.g. **again**, **said**) which your child will be learning in his or her first few years at school.

A few other words have been used to help the stories to flow.

Reading the book

1 Make sure you and your child are sitting in a quiet, comfortable place.

2 Tell him or her a little about the stories, without giving too much away:

In the first story, you can help to find the Zebrapotamus!

A favourite cat jumps and dances his way through the second story.

A little girl has some wonderful dreams in the third story, but she's quite pleased when she wakes up.

Someone is very grumpy in the last story!

This will give your child a mental picture; having a context for a story makes it easier to read the words.

3 Read the target words (above) together. This will mean that you can both enjoy the stories without having to spend too much time working out the words. Help your child to sound out each word (e.g. **h-i-ll**) before saying the whole word.

4 Let your child read the stories aloud. Help him or her with any difficult words and discuss the stories as you go along. Stop now and again to ask your child to predict what will happen next. This will help you to see whether he or she has understood what has happened so far.

Above all, enjoy the stories, and praise your child's reading!

Ruth Miskin's

Superphonics

Green Storybook

The
Zebrapotamus

by Gill Munton

Illustrated by Neal Layton

Hodder
Children's
Books

a division of Hachette Children's Books

The Zebrapotamus

Look! In the treetop!

Count, one, two.

Do you see him?

"Yes, we do!"

Look! In the long grass,

Going up the hill,

Will we catch him?

"Yes, we will!"

Is he a pandapin?

A wallaphant?

"No!"

A terrabat?

A buffacat?

"No, no, no!"

"Let me tell you who I am.

I'm not one of the things you said.

I am Zebrapotamus ...

... and now I'm going to bed!"

It's that cat again!

Who's that sitting in my hat?

Who's that playing on the mat?

Who's that asking for a pat?

It's that cat again!

Who's that jumping on my bed?

Who's that dancing on the shed?

Who's that wanting to be fed?

It's that cat again!

Who's that going **nip, nip, nip?**

Who's that going *rip, rip, rip?*

Who's that asking for a chip?

It's that cat again!

Who's that jumping on a rag?

Who's that playing a game of tag?

Who's that looking in my bag?

It's that cat again!

Who's that going to the vet?

Who's that getting very wet?

Who's my very, very best pet?

It's that cat again!

Wishing

I wish I had a pirate ship.

I'd strut along the deck,

With a hook for a hand,

and a patch on one eye,

And gold around my neck ...

I wish I had a book of spells,
And a tall black witch's hat,
And a bat and a frog
  and some cobwebs,
And a little witch's cat ...

I wish I had an elephant,

With wrinkly, crinkly skin,

And a wrinkly, crinkly,

  trumpety trunk

To keep his sandwiches in ...

I wish I had a pop star mum,

With a glass of fizz to sip,

Singing in a top girl band,

Her hand upon her hip ...

I'm glad I'm not a pirate.

Those pirates really pong!

I don't like witches any more.

(And all my spells went wrong!)

An elephant isn't much of a pet.

That trunk gives a nasty whack!

And as for mums - I think I'm glad ...

... I've got my old one back!

The big grump

I'm cross, I'm mad, I'm angry.

I've really got the hump.

I don't want to come and play.

I'm just a great big grump.

I want to yell and slam the door.

I want to chuck a brick.

I don't want to come and play.

Playing makes me sick.

I want to sit here by myself.

I want to stamp and slump.

I don't want to come and play.

I'm just a great big grump.

I'm gruff, I'm grim, I'm grizzly.

I'm kicking up a stink.

I don't want to come and play.

I want to sit and think ...

... I think I'm feeling happy now!

I want to run and jump!

Wait for me! I want to play!

Who called me a great big grump?